This book belongs to:

Eeyore's Happy Tail

Disney's Out & About With Pooh
A Grow and Learn Library

Published by Advance Publishers
© 1996 Disney Enterprises, Inc.
Based on the Pooh stories by A. A. Milne © The Pooh Properties Trust.
All rights reserved. Printed in the United States.
No part of this book may be reproduced or copied in any form
without written permission from the copyright owner.

Written by Ronald Kidd
Illustrated by Arkadia Illustration Ltd.
Designed by Vickey Bolling
Produced by Bumpy Slide Books

ISBN: 1-885222-60-2
10 9 8 7 6 5 4 3 2 1

Eyore was laughing — and his friends were laughing, too, gathered in a jolly group all around him. They loved his jokes. They loved his songs. They loved the way he would drop everything and do a little dance — because that's just the sort of donkey he was.

Everyone loved spending time with Eeyore. Wherever he went, fun wasn't far behind.

Eeyore opened his eyes. He was sitting in a thistle patch, all alone. The jolly group had been a dream. So had the jokes and songs and dances. And instead of feeling happy, Eeyore was quite sad — because that's just the sort of donkey he was.

He closed his eyes again, hoping the happy Eeyore would come back. Sure enough, he did hear someone laughing.

"Hello, there, Eeyore!" called a voice.
Opening his eyes, he saw Tigger bouncing toward him.
"Beee-yooo-tiful day, isn't it?" said Tigger.
Eeyore replied, "I suppose it is, for some."

Tigger bounced up and down, wearing a big grin. Eeyore watched him closely. He thought that if he looked hard enough, perhaps he could see what made Tigger so happy. That's when he noticed Tigger's tail. It was a cheerful, crinkly sort of tail. When Tigger bounced, it folded up like an accordion and sent him flying toward the sky.

Eeyore looked back at his own tail. It didn't fold up. It didn't crinkle. It just hung there.

"Well, there you have it," he said.
"There you have what?" asked Tigger.
"A tail," Eeyore replied. "A very sad tail."

Tigger went around to the other end of Eeyore and looked at his tail. "I think I see the problem," he reported back. "We'll have you fixed up in no time."

He gave Eeyore's tail a good crinkling. Then he folded it up and called out to Eeyore, "Okay, you're all set. Now lean back, and before you know it, you'll be bouncin', just like me!"

Eeyore leaned back. "Am I bouncing yet?" he asked, trying to contain his excitement.

"Almost," said Tigger.

Eeyore leaned farther and farther back. For a moment he thought he felt a bounce coming on.

Then, all at once, he really did feel something.

It was the ground. He had fallen over.

Eeyore looked up at his friend. "Thank you for your help, Tigger," he said. "But I don't think my tail was meant for bouncing."

"Then what was it meant for?" asked Tigger.
It was a question Eeyore couldn't answer. But he thought he knew someone who could.

In another part of the forest, Owl was talking about his favorite subject: great owls in history. Pooh sat nearby, trying to listen, but it reminded him of his favorite subject: great honey pots in history. He was about to go looking

for one when Eeyore came plodding down the path.

"Owl," said Eeyore, "I have an important question. It has to do with tails."

"Tails?" said Owl. "I've got just the thing."

Owl went into his house and came out holding a big book. It was called *Tails Around the World*.

Clearing his throat, Owl said, "You see, tails are some of the most interesting things in the animal kingdom. Different tails are used in different ways. For instance, my great-uncle Herman . . ."

A long while later, Owl said, "Now, did someone have a question?"

"I think Eeyore did," said Pooh. "But it's hard to remember back that far."

Eeyore, who had been waiting patiently, said, "As you know, Owl, my tail is rather sad and droopy. Is there anything I can do to make it a happy tail?"

"Excellent question!" said Owl.

He opened the book and flipped through the pages. "Happy tails, happy tails . . . Ah, yes, here we are. One of the happiest tails in the animal kingdom is a dog's tail. It wags back and forth whenever the dog is excited."

Eeyore liked the idea of wagging his tail. He asked the others to step back and give him room. Then he did some stretching exercises to make sure he wouldn't hurt himself.

Finally he took a deep breath and wagged. He wagged every part of his body that he could. The one part that didn't wag was his tail.

Pooh reached over and tried to wag Eeyore's tail for him, but somehow it wasn't the same. "Perhaps wagging isn't the answer," said Pooh.

Owl nodded and turned to another page in his book. "The beaver also has a happy tail. It's long and flat, like a paddle. He uses it to pound mud and sticks together when he builds his home."

Eeyore thought that pounding was a fine way to use his tail. He led Owl and Pooh down to the edge of the stream. Gathering up some sticks, he set them on the muddy bank beneath his tail and tried to pound them. But what his tail did wasn't exactly pounding. It was more like flapping in the breeze. Eeyore just sighed.

Owl flipped through the book once again. "Here's another happy tail," he said. "A monkey tail is almost like a hand. The monkey uses it to hang from branches and swing through the trees."

Eeyore imagined himself swinging through the trees by his tail. He almost smiled just thinking about it. Maybe a monkey tail was exactly what he needed.

Eeyore wrapped his tail around a tree branch. Then he closed his eyes and concentrated on swinging through the tree like a monkey.

After a while Eeyore opened his eyes. "Well, I'll be," he said, looking down, "Owl and Pooh look just like ants."

But what Eeyore was seeing *were* ants, because he had never left the ground.

Owl flipped through his book and said, "Here's another happy tail."

"I don't know if I can stand much more happiness," Eeyore said.

"This one is perfect," said Owl. "You don't wag it or pound it or swing on it. All you do is walk around and let people admire it. It's a peacock tail."

Owl went into his house and got a fan. He pinned it to Eeyore's tail and spread it out so all the colors showed.

PEACOCK

"There you have it," said Owl proudly. "Now you have a happy tail."

Pooh said, "Eeyore, you must be very . . . well, happy."

"You know," Eeyore said, glancing back at his new tail, "I think maybe I am."

Eeyore spent the rest of the morning admiring his reflection in the pond. When he grew tired of that, he went to see his friend Christopher Robin.

Christopher Robin was sitting under an oak tree with Pooh, Piglet, and Tigger. He looked up and said, "My goodness, I didn't know we had a peacock in the forest!"

"Christopher Robin, I'm not a peacock," said the old donkey. "I'm Eeyore."

Christopher Robin said, "I'm sorry, but you can't be Eeyore. Eeyore's tail is sad and droopy. That's one of the things I love about him."

"It is?" said Eeyore.

Eeyore looked at Christopher Robin, then at his new tail. Slowly he reached around and took off the fan.

"Eeyore, it really *is* you!" said Christopher Robin, giving him a big hug. "I'm glad that you're back."

"So am I," said Eeyore.

Pooh, Piglet, and Tigger came up beside Christopher Robin. Smiling and laughing, they formed a jolly group, almost like the one in Eeyore's dream. And even though he didn't joke, or sing, or do a little dance, Eeyore felt happy, because he had friends who loved him just the way he was.